The Surprise at Blowcart Beach

A Challenge Island STEAM Adventure

By Sharon Duke Estroff and Joel Ross

Illustrated by Mónica de Rivas

WEST
MARGIN
PRESS

Library of Congress Cataloging-in-Publication Data

Names: Estroff, Sharon, author. | Ross, Joel N., 1968- author. | DeRivas, Mónica, illustrator.
Title: The surprise at Blowcart Beach : a challenge island STEAM adventure / by Sharon Duke Estroff and Joel Ross ; illustrated by Mónica de Rivas.
Description: Berkeley : West Margin Press, [2023] | Series: Challenge island ; book 3 | Audience: Ages 7-10. | Audience: Grades 2-3. | Summary: Daniel, Joy, and Kimani appear on a beach and see a mysterious tower in the distance, but to reach the tower in time, they must work together and build a cart for speed with the materials they have on hand.
Identifiers: LCCN 2022016225 (print) | LCCN 2022016226 (ebook) | ISBN 9781513134949 (paperback) | ISBN 9781513134956 (hardback) | ISBN 9781513134963 (ebook)
Subjects: CYAC: Beaches--Fiction. | Cooperativeness--Fiction. | Resourcefulness--Fiction. | Problem solving--Fiction.
Classification: LCC PZ7.1.E854 Su 2022 (print) | LCC PZ7.1.E854 (ebook) | DDC [Fic]--dc23
LC record available at https://lccn.loc.gov/2022016225
LC ebook record available at https://lccn.loc.gov/2022016226

Printed in China
27 26 25 24 23 1 2 3 4 5

Published by West Margin Press®

WEST
MARGIN
PRESS
WestMarginPress.com

Proudly distributed by Ingram Publisher Services

WEST MARGIN PRESS

Publishing Director: Jennifer Newens
Marketing Manager: Alice Wertheimer
Project Specialist: Micaela Clark

Editor: Olivia Ngai
Design & Production: Rachel Lopez Metzger

Dear Reader,

Welcome to Challenge Island, a magical place where engineering meets imagination! You are about to set sail on an exhilarating voyage to one of the many action-packed Challenge Islands. Each island comes with a unique set of problems that the Challenge Island kids have to solve—together! They have to be creative, using only what's in the treasure chest and their imaginations. After the story, at the back of the book, you will have a chance to try out the challenges with your own team at home!

Boom. Boom. Boom. Did you hear that? It sounds like the Challenge Island drums calling you. That means the adventure is about to begin. *Boom. Bada-boom!* There it is again. Sounds like it's time for us to get going full STEAM ahead!

Happy reading!
Sharon Duke Estroff
Co-Author and Founder/
CEO of the Challenge Island STEAM Program

Chapter 1

The passengers swayed as the subway squealed to a halt. They were packed in tight, so Daniel had to be extra careful not to smoosh the bakery box he was carrying. His grandma had sent him and Joy home with two doughnuts... though there was only one left.

The doors slid open. Daniel stepped out onto the platform and reached into the box for the last doughnut.

Chocolate-glazed, his favorite.

But before he grabbed it, Joy darted past, knocking his elbow.

"Watch out," he said.

"This is it!" Joy stood in the middle of the platform and spread her arms wide. "This is the spot!"

"Even more than the school bathrooms?" Daniel asked as the train rumbled away.

"Definitely! I told you I'd find the least magical-islandy place in the whole city."

"'Islandy' isn't a word."

"Island-ish, then," Joy said. "And I *also* told you that even in the least magical place, I can still do a trick."

Daniel snorted. "You cannot."

"Sure I can. Look at the train."

Daniel turned to watch the train disappear into the tunnel. "It's gone."

"That's my trick. Abracadabra—it vanished!"

"That's not magic. Magic is..." He started for the stairs that led up to the street. "It's zooming across the world in two seconds, from a snowy playground to a sunny beach."

"Or from an elevator into a rainforest?" Joy asked,

trotting beside him.

Daniel smiled, because that's exactly what had happened to them. Twice now they'd been summoned to a tropical island with their friend Kimani to face new adventures and tests. Not tests like school, though: tests like challenges. And both times, they'd passed... barely.

"What if we mess up the next time we're called to the island?" he asked Joy, taking the doughnut from the box and smelling its fudgy sweetness.

"We've messed up *every* time!" she said. "Can I have a bite?"

"You already ate yours."

"Which is exactly why I need a bite of yours."

"Just one," he said, handing her the doughnut.

She took a bite, and with her mouth full said, "Remember what Captain Wei said?"

Captain Wei was the mysterious drummer who had summoned them to the island with a magical drumbeat. Joy thought she was a pirate captain too, but Daniel wasn't so sure.

He made a face. "She said there's a greater challenge waiting for us."

"Would you stop worrying about that?"

"I'm not worried."

"You're worried-*ish*," Joy told him. "And I meant, do you remember what she said about messing up? She said we're good at working together to solve problems because we keep trying and failing until finally something works."

"So we're *good* at messing up?"

"The best!" She gestured wildly with Daniel's doughnut. "That's why—hey!"

A texting teenager bumped into her, knocking the doughnut from her hand before vanishing into the crowd.

"Oops," Joy said.

"Well, *that* was a failure," Daniel said, watching his doughnut roll across the floor, leaving a trail of chocolate glaze.

"It wasn't my fault!" Joy told him. "And you know I'm right. We and Kimani make a great team."

That was true. The three of them each had special strengths. Joy was energetic and fearless, and knew how to tie a million knots. Kimani was smart and organized, and wrote things in her little notebook. And Daniel was athletic and cautious and, uh... good at making friends with parrots?

"I guess," he said, tromping toward the stairs. "But Captain Wei really did say there's a bigger challenge waiting for us."

"Yeah," Joy said. "I can't wait."

"Just as long as there aren't any more monster snakes."

"Ooh! Do you think there'll be penguins next time?"

Daniel stopped midway up the stairs, in a patch of the daylight that streamed into the subway station from the street. He stared at Joy. "On a tropical island? No."

The crowd bustled around them. A bunch of businesswomen, their shoes going *click-clack-click*. A man with a cane, *tink-tunk-tink*. An older couple carrying shopping bags, *thup, swish, thup*.

"Then how about hoverboards?" Joy asked.

"Oh, sure," Daniel said. "There will probably be penguins *riding* hoverboards."

"Don't be silly," Joy said. "Penguins can't..."

She trailed off when the *click-swish-tunk* sounds of the crowd changed.

Boom-badoom-doom-boom-ba-BOOM.

Boom!

Boom-badoom-doom-boom-ba-BOOM.

"Boom!" Joy yelled, grabbing Daniel's arm. "Hold onto your haircut—here we go!"

The drumbeat pounded faster, fierce and happy, echoing through the train tunnel. The daylight at the top of the stairs glowed brighter and brighter, and the air suddenly smelled of ocean breezes.

Boom-badoom-doom-boom-ba-BOOM.

Then the drums *whooshed* them away.

Daniel felt himself swooping upward like sparks rising from a campfire. The subway station disappeared, and

Daniel fell—down, down, down!

He landed on his feet, gentle as butterfly's whisper. He was standing beside Joy in the dark. He could make out the inside of a cave with brilliant sunlight pouring through an opening in front of them.

Daniel blinked and saw a shadow in the brilliant light. A huge figure, silhouetted against the sun.

Like a troll or a cyclops... that turned toward them and let loose a cry.

Chapter 2

"There you are!" the figure said.

"K-Kimani?" Daniel asked as his vision adjusted to the brightness.

"Of course!" Kimani laughed and stepped forward. She was wearing her purple backpack again—the one she always kept her notebook in—and a red headband. "Who were you expecting?"

Joy ran forward to hug Kimani. "You know Daniel! When he sees light at the end of a tunnel, he figures it's an oncoming train."

Which actually made more sense than a cyclops, so Daniel just said, "At least I didn't shout, 'Hang onto your haircut.'"

"What?" Joy looked over her shoulder. "It's a saying."

"The saying is 'hang onto your hat.'"

"You aren't wearing a hat."

"That doesn't matter! It's still not a saying."

"Anything you say is a saying," Joy said. "That's what 'saying' means!"

"You two are *exactly* the same!" Kimani laughed. "And Joy's right that you're not wearing a hat, Daniel. But you *are* wearing a headband."

"Oh!" He reached up and touched the cloth. "So are you, Joy."

Joy crossed her eyes trying to look at her own forehead. "What color's mine?"

"Red, same as Kimani's. That's why I didn't see it at first—it blends in with your fiery head."

"All our headbands are red because we're on the same team," Joy told him. "And *look*! We're in a cave!"

Kimani said, "I was wondering when you'd notice."

"I already did," Daniel said, even though he hadn't seen much with the sun shining so brightly behind Kimani.

Now he looked closer. The cave was about the size of a classroom. Patches of sand filled the lowest places in the rocky floor while vines swayed in the breeze around the wide, bright entrance where the sun was shining through. Daniel heard the crash of surf and the cry of seagulls and realized the cave must be near a beach.

He turned away from the mouth of the cave and noticed crates and barrels lining the walls of the cave. There were dozens of them, some open and some closed, along with rough planks, wagon wheels, and broken oil lanterns.

"Whoa," he said. "This is like a s—"

"Smuggler's cave!" Kimani said. "I know!"

"I was going to say supply closet," he said.

"Except instead of mops," Kimani said, "there are hundred-year-old crates and barrels... and an ancient parchment with scribbled notes."

Daniel opened his mouth to ask a question, but Kimani kept talking.

"There's all *kinds* of weird stuff," she said. "That barrel behind you is overflowing with rusty horseshoes, and the one next to that is full of moldy cloth."

"They're not all old," Joy said from where she was climbing a pile of crates. "Some look—"

"Would you get down from there?" Daniel called to Joy, forgetting what he'd been going to ask Kimani. "What if you twist an ankle?"

"That's why I've got two." Joy plopped down on a crate and peered at the small barrel beside her. "Some of these look pretty new. Like this one says... ha!"

"What does it say?" Kimani asked.

"Supplies!" Joy announced.

Kimani smiled. "So Daniel was right!"

"For once," Joy said. "Do you think Captain Wei zapped all this stuff here?"

"She said she can't control the island's magic," Kimani said, "so probably not. But she was definitely in this cave."

Joy drummed her fingers on the crate beneath her. "How can you tell?"

"Check out those drawings." Kimani nodded to a few dozen sketches tacked to one of the biggest crates. "They're all pictures of pirate ships."

Daniel peered closer, then told Joy, "From huge ones with three masts to little ones with a single mast."

"I think the ships are called different things depending on the number of sails they have," Kimani said. "Like sloops and schooners and brigs."

"'Sloop' isn't a real word!" Joy hopped down from the crates. "But yeah, it does seem like Captain Wei was here."

"There's even a couple paintings on canvas, like in a

museum," Kimani said, gesturing to the cave wall. Two paintings were propped against it, half-hidden by the crate. One was about the size of a TV screen and showed a sailboat speeding across a lake. The other was five times bigger... and showed a bunch of sailboats speeding across the same lake.

"Looks like a race," Daniel said. "The sails are full of wind... what's that word? Not bellowing."

"Billowing?" Kimani suggested.

"That's the one," Daniel said.

"Pirate captains do like speed," Joy said.

Kimani straightened her headband. "I bet the tide carries flotsam and jetsam here from around the world. That's why there's so much stuff on the island."

"What're flotsam and jetsam?" Daniel asked.

"Jetsam is anything floating in the ocean that people threw overboard on purpose. Flotsam is stuff that's floating in the ocean because of an accident or a wreck."

"You know what they say," Joy said, running her fingers

along a low plank holding copper bowls and dented buckets. "You flot some, you jet some."

Daniel groaned, then brightened. "Look, there are some poles leaning against the back wall. Bamboo, like the first time we came to this island! I guess those are flotsam if they fell in the water by accident?"

"Right," Kimani said.

"And jetsam is—" He stopped as he remembered what he'd been going to ask her. "Wait a second! Did you say 'an ancient parchment with a note'?"

Kimani smiled. "I wondered if you heard that! Yeah, I was poking around before you two got here and found—"

"A poem!" Joy interrupted.

"Close," Kimani said, and pointed to a scrap of paper tacked among the sketches of ships. "But instead of a poem, I found that."

Chapter 3

"That's not a poem?" Daniel asked when he saw old-fashioned writing on the paper.

"Not exactly," Kimani said, and read aloud:

Your task is simple, my brave crew:

Cross the dunes with barrels of glue

Or nails or sails—it's yours to choose!

But watch for sands that trap and ooze.

Sail to my tower soon or else,

This island chain will...

Will...

Will...

Drat! I can't think of a word that rhymes with "else." Well, come to my tower with a few of the barrels from this cave. If you succeed, we'll meet again—and I'll tell you more!

Onward to the challenge,

Captain Wei

Joy laughed. "She couldn't think of a rhyme!"

"At least we understand the challenge this time," Daniel said. "Bring a few barrels to her tower. Simple."

"Simple doesn't mean easy," Kimani said.

"Belse," Joy said.

Daniel frowned. "Huh?"

"Nothing," Joy said, then continued to mutter. "Pelse, shelse, grelse..."

"She's trying to think of a rhyme for 'else,'" Kimani explained to Daniel. "C'mon, let's look around."

When Daniel followed her to the mouth of the cave,

the wind ruffled his hair. He blinked at the sunlight then stepped outside onto a flat patch of ground.

The cave opened partway up a cliffside that loomed behind him. A wide, sandy path led from the mouth of the cave down toward a little stretch of coastline. Curling white-tipped waves lapped onto a beach where a flock of birds chased the tide, poking their pointy bills into the sand.

The sun felt hot on his face despite the blowing wind. He scanned the ocean for dolphin fins but didn't see any, so he squinted at the other islands rising in the distance.

"Where's the tower?" he asked.

"What?" Kimani yelled. She had already started down the path and couldn't hear him over the wind.

When she turned, Daniel saw that her T-shirt said, *HOW'S MY READING? Call 1-800-TELL-ME-AFTER-I-FINISH-THIS-CHAPTER.*

"Where's the tower?" he repeated.

"I don't know," Kimani said. "Maybe we can see it from the beach."

"Last one there's a rotten else!" Joy shouted from behind as she charged downhill past them.

"A rotten *else*?" Daniel said.

Kimani didn't hear him again—this time because she was chasing Joy toward the beach.

"Hey!" he yelled after them.

To his surprise, Joy didn't tease him when he reached the beach last. She just pointed into the distance along the

coastline and said, "Look."

The wind whipping off the ocean pulled strands of red hair from her ponytail. They flew forward, like her hair was pointing too—pointing *everywhere*. Toward the ocean and the sky and the sand, toward the rainforest that rose high and green along the coast of the island they were on.

But her finger pointed toward a grassy hill that stood across what looked like a mile of the widest, lumpiest,

bumpiest beach ever. White boulders dotted the hillside and a round stone tower rose from the top. Windows spiraled up the outside wall of the tower, and a carpet of yellow flowers led uphill between the boulders toward what looked like a door.

"That's the way in," Joy said.

Daniel nodded. "So we just need to lug a couple of barrels across the beach, and we're done!"

"That's a lot of beach," Kimani said.

"Yeah," Daniel said. "And the barrels look heavy."

"I saw a few small ones," Joy said. "Like the size of buckets. We can totally carry them."

"Then let's get lugging," Daniel said, turning back toward the cave.

"Ooh, there are streams between some of those dunes," Joy said behind him.

"Flowing from the rainforest to the ocean?" Kimani asked. "I really need to sketch this."

"After you help with the barrels!" Daniel shouted,

already at the mouth of the cave.

He didn't hear an answer because of the wind, so he just trotted inside. He blinked for a few seconds, waiting for his eyes to adjust to the darkness. Then he reached for a small, empty barrel with a wagon wheel propped nearby.

His dad always told him to lift with his legs, not his back, so he squatted low.

Even though the barrel was small and empty, it was pretty solid. He wrapped his arms around the damp wood. He exhaled, lifted a few inches, and—

"Don't move that!" Kimani cried behind him.

Chapter 4

Daniel grunted. "Why not?"

Moving the barrels was the whole point!

Except Kimani didn't mean the barrel. She meant the wagon wheel that he'd nudged over a few inches when he had bent down.

The wagon wheel fell against *another* wagon wheel that fell against another one. And that one smacked a fourth one, which wobbled slowly across the uneven ground, directly toward the plank-shelf balanced on a crate stacked with seashells and copper bowls.

The wheel tapped the plank about as a hard as you tap the space bar on a computer. And for a second, nothing else happened.

Then the plank see-sawed, flinging bowls and shells across the cave! It swiveled into the pyramid stack of barrels, which crashed with a tremendous clamor of splintering wood and clanging brass.

When the dust cleared, Daniel gaped at the cave floor, strewn with broken barrels, rusted metal, and waterlogged cloth.

"Oh," he said, his shoulders slumping. "That's why."

"Are you okay?" Kimani asked.

"Yeah," he muttered, his cheeks hot with embarrassment.

Joy peered at the ruins from the opening of the cave where she still stood. "That actually helped, Daniel. Now there's only a few barrels to choose from."

"Mostly the small ones," Kimani said, wading into the wreckage. "I guess they're stronger."

"Small things rule," Joy said as she made her way to them.

"We can't use barrels that will fall apart anyway," Kimani told Daniel.

"I guess," he muttered, but he felt a little better.

"Here's a smaller one,'" Joy said, after rummaging around.

"The perfect size for you," Daniel told her.

She wrinkled her nose. "It's labeled twenty-five pounds."

"Just don't throw it on the ground like you did with my doughnut!"

"That wasn't my fault," Joy said.

"It was too," Daniel said. Then he added, "Remember to lift with your legs."

Kimani dragged a wagon wheel out of the way and said, "I'll try the barrel that says 'supplies.' It's smaller too."

"Maybe it's full of feathers," Joy said. "Bird supplies."

Kimani tilted the barrel, then grunted. "It's not that light." She looked closer at the label. "Oh! It's glue, like it said in the poem. We're definitely taking this one."

"Glue is like 'else,'" Joy told her. "Nothing rhymes with glue."

Kimani stared at her. "Blue, flew, true, you..."

"Well, *almost* nothing," Joy said, and lifted her barrel with a groan.

Daniel and Kimani switched places. He hugged the glue barrel to his chest while she grabbed the empty barrel. After all, the poem said they could choose what barrels to bring; it didn't say they needed to be full! He staggered into the sunlight, careful not to trip on the rough ground.

Climbing down the windy path was a hundred times harder with a barrel of glue in his arms. Still, he powered onward until he reached the beach. He lowered the barrel and collapsed, panting and sweating like he'd sprinted the one-mile run at school.

The waves crashed, the wind blew. A few birds sang in rainforest that rose alongside the beach, but he was too tired to look for DaVinci the parrot, who they had met the other times they were brought to the island.

"Watch out!" Joy yelled.

Daniel looked over his shoulder and saw her small

barrel was speeding out of control—rolling directly toward him. It was moving fast, like a bowling ball about to crash into the pins.

He yelped and dove out of the way—and Joy's barrel jounced wildly, veering off to the side before half-burying itself in the sand.

"Well, rolling doesn't help," Joy announced as she trotted past.

Kimani flopped down beside Daniel, gasping for breath. "Okay, so... we tried that. Now can we... think of a better way?"

"But we're almost there," Daniel said, wiping sweat from his face with his headband. "It's only one tiny mile away."

"Are you kidding?" Kimani asked, gaping at him. "I can't carry this another ten feet, forget about—"

Daniel grinned.

Kimani laughed. "Oh, you *are* kidding!"

"Well, now we know one way that doesn't work," he said.

"Isn't that what Joy's dad always says?" Kimani asked.

"Not always," Joy said, dragging her barrel back toward

them. "Only when my plans don't work."

"So ten times a day," Daniel said.

Joy stuck out her tongue. "Well, I've got a perfect plan now."

"What's that?"

"Search the rainforest!" She ran toward the trees, her sneakers sending arcs of beach sand behind her. "I'll look for ziplines or hoverboards!"

Kimani looked at Daniel. "Hoverboards?"

"Just don't get her started on penguins," he said.

"I love penguins!" Kimani said. "Did you know that a group of penguins is called a raft if they're in the water, but a waddle if they're on land?"

He eyed her. "Now *I* can't tell if *you're* kidding."

"It's true," she said, just as terrible shrieking sounded from the forest.

Chapter 5

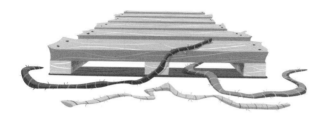

A flock of black birds with orange beaks erupted from the trees as the shrieks came louder and faster.

Daniel jumped to his feet. The screaming sounded like a hundred angry goblins marching to war. His heart squeezed tight—until he spotted Joy racing back toward them.

"What *is* that?" he called.

"I didn't stick around to find out!" she yelled, running closer.

Daniel looked at Kimani. "What're you smiling about?"

"That's just monkeys—like last time we were in the rainforest here. Don't you remember?"

"Oh, right." Daniel exhaled. "They are kind of scary."

"It's just monkeys?" Joy looked back toward the forest. "I'm not scared of them."

"What about the anaconda?" Daniel shuddered as he thought about the giant snake that had lurked in the swamp. "She's in there too, you know."

"On second thought," Joy said, "let's stick to the beach."

"Okay," Daniel told Kimani. "We tried moving the barrels my way and we tried it Joy's way—now would you tell us the *right* way?"

"I don't know the right way!" Kimani said.

"Take a guess."

"Um, we could build some sort of vehicle? Like a sled?"

"That sounds right," Daniel said. "There are ropes and stuff in the cave."

Joy nodded. "We can put the barrels on the sled and drag them."

As they headed back toward the cave, the wind blew stinging sand against Daniel's face. He closed his eyes to slits—then stopped. "Wait, what about the ocean?"

"It's still right there," Joy said.

"Yeah," he said. "I know where the ocean is, Joy."

"He means what about a building a raft," Kimani told her. "But I'm not sure how we'd float or steer. And the poem says to cross the *dunes*."

"Plus the tower's not right on the beach," Joy said. "So we'd have to lug the barrels anyway."

"Okay, a sled it is then," Daniel said.

"We'll need a flat board," Kimani said, "and some ropes to pull it."

They rummaged around the cave until Kimani found near the back wall a big rectangle of heavy wooden slats attached to three cross-pieces.

"This is perfect for a sled," she said. "I guess it's the broken-off bottom of a crate?"

"It's called a pallet," Daniel told her.

"What's it for?" Kimani asked.

Daniel was proud that he finally knew something Kimani didn't. "Workers use them in warehouses to move things around with forklifts."

"Really? Neat." Kimani examined the pallet carefully. "I'm going to have to write that down."

"I found some ropes," Joy said, and tied them to one edge of the pallet.

The three of them started dragging the heavy pallet outside like a team of dogs pulling a sled across the snow. Except snow is slippery, and the cave floor was not. Scraping the pallet across the ground was difficult, even without the weight of the barrels on it.

"This is almost as bad as carrying everything," Daniel said.

"Yeah," Joy said. "Stupid friction."

"Luckily, I know exactly what to do," Daniel said.

Kimani tugged her ponytail. "What's that?"

"Isn't it obvious? I'm going to wait for *you* to think of something better."

Joy grinned and told Kimani, "Take your time, though. There's no rush. We *probably* won't get sent home before we meet Captain Wei again and—"

"I already thought of something," Kimani said.

"Ha!" Daniel said. "I knew you would."

Joy tilted her head. "Does it involve hoverboards?"

"Close," Kimani told Joy. "We'll build a cart."

Chapter 6

"The wagon wheels!" Daniel said, catching on to Kimani's idea to move the barrels. "We can attach them to one of the crates and put the barrels inside."

"The crates are too small," Kimani said. "Let's stick with the pallet—and use the bamboo poles as axles."

"Which are, um..." He tried to remember the picture book about trucks that his dad used to read him. "The poles that connect wheels to a car?"

"Exactly," Kimani said.

While Daniel cleared a workspace in the middle of the

cave, Kimani gathered bamboo poles and wheels, and Joy dug through the wreckage for more rope. Then Daniel and Kimani lifted one end of the pallet at a time while Joy slid the bamboo poles beneath.

"They stick out, like, five feet on each side," Joy said after she finished.

"That's okay," Daniel told her. "As long as can we can fit through the cave opening. But how're we going to attach the poles—um, the axles—to the pallet—um, the cart?"

"There are notches on the bottom of the pallet," Kimani said. "I guess for a forklift? Those notches will keep the axles in place."

"Ooh," Joy said, "and I can use the horseshoes too!" She reached into a barrel and pulled out a few horseshoes. Then she turned the horseshoes to point upward like capital U's and tied them to the pallet—two in the front, two in the rear—at the notches with rope. Kimani slid the bamboo poles through the notches and horseshoes, making sure the poles were still loose enough to twirl freely round and

round. Finally, Daniel popped the wheels on the ends. He slid each wheel along a pole for a few feet until it reached a thicker section of the bamboo, then he jammed it into place.

They took a step back to look at their creation.

"That actually worked," Kimani said, sounding surprised.

Daniel grinned. "Awesome, right? In a cave, on a tropical island—"

"Using only flotsam and jetsam," Kimani continued, "we built a cart."

"A *go*-cart!" Joy said, hopping up on the pallet. "So what're you waiting for, Daniel? It's not a called a *stay*-cart. Push me!"

"I'll check if everything's okay outside." Kimani darted through the cave mouth, then yelled, "Looks good!"

"Here goes," Daniel said.

Joy shouted, "Go go go!"

Daniel grabbed the end of the pallet and shoved the cart toward the cave's opening. The wheels turned the axles, which spun in the horseshoes, which stayed in place on the pallet. The whole thing rolled unsteadily forward—but it rolled!

"Keep going," Joy shouted, then grabbed Daniel's shoulder. "Whoa! Bouncy."

"Sorry," Daniel started. "I'll try to—"

"I like bouncy! Faster, faster!"

He laughed and pushed the cart harder. The dented, warped wheels rasped across the rocky floor, crunching seashells and knocking aside bits of wood. Then one bamboo axle, sticking out a few feet from the wheel, scraped the side wall of the cave while another axle snagged on a broken crate before springing free.

"Almost there," Joy said.

Daniel couldn't steer the cart much, but he tried to aim for the middle of the mouth of the cave. The bamboo axles scraped against rock, then caught on something.

So he gave one last shove—and the cart squeezed through.

Chapter 7

Daniel grinned at the cart as it rolled out into the sunlight. He couldn't believe they'd done it. The wheels and axles actually worked!

He and Joy pushed the cart toward the beach while Kimani guided them from the front. The warped wheels wobbled on the bouncy axles, which wobbled on the battered pallet, which just... wobbled.

Daniel thought it was cool that they'd built a go-cart out of flotsam and jetpacks—or whatever Kimani called it—but it wasn't exactly a smooth ride.

As the cart creaked and shuddered down the path, Daniel's back started aching from bending over. Joy panted, then swallowed a mouthful of windblown sand, and Kimani smacked the pallet with her shin.

She hopped around swearing... except instead of swearing, she yelled, "Oh, caboose!" and "Shut-the-front-door," and "Pants!" like some kind of wacky cartoon character.

Then she noticed Daniel and Joy staring at her, and ducked her head. She looked so embarrassed that Daniel elbowed Joy, meaning, *Don't tease Kimani.*

They reached the beach a minute later. Pushing the cart was already pretty tough, but pushing it through sand was even tougher. Probably because of friction.

Still, they didn't have any choice, so they loaded the three barrels onto the pallet, then stood there looking across the rippling, sandy beach toward the tower.

Looking far across the rippling, sandy beach.

Far, far, *far* across the rippling, sandy beach.

"In the sand, this isn't much of a go-cart," Joy said. "It's more of a no-go-cart."

"Yeah, this is going to take us forever," Daniel said, plopping down on the edge of the pallet. "We need to get there before sunset."

"We must be missing something," Kimani said.

"A helicopter," Joy suggested.

"What're we missing?" Daniel asked.

"I don't know." Kimani pulled her notebook from her purple backpack. "What did the poem say again exactly?"

"I mostly remember the part about her not finishing the poem," Joy said.

"Me too," Daniel admitted.

Kimani flipped pages, then read aloud. "Cross the dunes with barrels of glue, or nails or sails—it's yours to choose!"

"That part is easy," Daniel said. "We have to cross the beach with a few barrels."

"But what about 'watch for sands that trap and ooze'?" Kimani tapped her notebook with a fingertip. "Maybe that's about the sand closer to the tower."

"Yeah, probably," Daniel said. "So what comes next?"

"Sail to my tower soon or else..." Kimani trailed off. "Hmm."

"Hmm what?"

Kimani frowned. "I wonder why she wrote 'sails' twice? First 'barrels of sails' and then 'sail to my tower...'"

"Because she's not very good at poems," Daniel said.

"Yeah," Joy said. "She's *Captain* Wei, not *Poet* Wei."

The wind blew harder, flapping the pages of Kimani's notebook before—

"Way!" a voice cried above them. "Way, way!"

Daniel caught sight of a yellow-and-blue parrot soaring above them and shouted, "DaVinci!"

"Pretty!" DaVinci squawked back. "Pretty DaVinci."

"You are pretty, you silly bird." Daniel patted his shoulder. "Come down!"

DaVinci spread his wings, but the wind grew stronger and lofted him upward. "Ahoy!" he called, faintly.

"That's the wrong direction!" Daniel yelled after him.

Joy shaded her eyes with her hand. "The wind's

carrying him away."

"Sails!" Kimani said, grabbing Daniel's arm.

"Huh?"

Her dark eyes shone. "The sketches in the cave."

"What about them?" he asked.

"They all showed pirate ships with billowing sails, right? Sails full of wind?"

Joy snickered. "Pirate 'sloops.'"

"Oh!" Daniel said as DaVinci was finally able to land on his shoulder.

"We're going to attach a sail to the go-cart," Kimani announced. "We're going to harness wind power."

"Wing power!" DaVinci said, his claws digging into Daniel's shoulder.

"Wind power," Daniel corrected.

"Wing power!" DaVinci said again.

"You're both right," Joy said. "We're going to *sail* across the beach!"

Chapter 8

"Just one small problem," Daniel said. "We need a sail."

"That's not a problem." Joy started for the cave. "There's plenty of cloth and rope back at the cave. We'll make a sail!"

"What if—" Daniel started, but Joy was already gone. So he turned to Kimani. "Won't we need to sew to make a sail? I didn't see a needle and thread."

"Yeah, and we're supposed to reach the tower 'soon,'" Kimani said.

"Maybe we missed something inside," Daniel said as he followed Joy. "Like a kite."

"Abaft the beam!" DaVinci squawked.

"Or a beam," Kimani said.

DaVinci happily chirped from Daniel's shoulder, then flew away when Daniel stepped inside the cave.

"Help me unravel this," Joy called from the darkness.

Daniel spotted her in the middle of the cave where she was wrestling with a roll of cloth taller than she was.

"It smells like anchovies," he said, walking over and taking a corner of the moldy cloth.

"All the best sails are made of anchovies," Joy informed him.

"Sails are usually made from canvas," Kimani said, making a face as she grabbed another section of the cloth.

"Wait." Joy tilted her head. "Canvas?"

"Yeah, why?"

Joy dropped the cloth. "Ha! This time I realized something before you two!"

"Realized what?" Daniel asked.

Joy gestured to the two sailboat paintings that were

leaning against the cave wall. "Ta-da! Canvas!"

"Oh, that's right!" Daniel said. "Kimani said those paintings are on canvas."

"I totally forgot about that," Kimani said. "Maybe we can use a painting for the sail."

She grabbed the smaller, TV screen–sized painting while Daniel chose a bamboo pole for a mast. He thought for a second, then picked up a jagged length of wood from a broken crate too. Joy loaded her arms with ropes and they headed outside to the cart.

Kimani held the painting sideways to the wind, but a strong gust almost yanked it from her grip. She yelped in surprise and twisted it away from the wind, then managed to stagger the rest of the way to the cart.

Daniel used his piece of broken crate like a spear to pry a hole between the slats on the top and bottom of the pallet. Then he and Kimani tilted the cart slightly—which was tough with the axles sticking out—and shoved the bamboo mast into the hole so that it stood upright on the pallet.

While Joy tied a bunch of knots to keep the mast in place, Daniel broke off the side pieces of the frame holding the canvas. Now there was just a piece of wood along the top and the bottom holding the canvas in a square shape.

"Hey, you made yardarms," Kimani said.

"*What* arms?" Daniel asked.

"Yardarms are the poles that attach a square-rigged sail to the mast."

"Why don't you get your yardarms over here and help me?" Daniel said as he poked holes at the top and the bottom of the painting. Kimani lifted the canvas and slid it onto bamboo mast through the holes. Lastly, Joy tied the yardarms to the mast with a bunch more knots.

Daniel hefted the barrels back up onto the pallet. The ocean breeze whipped against their new sail... and pushed the painting sideways, so it couldn't catch the wind.

"I'll stand at the mast and keep the sail straight when the wind hits it," Kimani said as she climbed on the cart. "Daniel, give us a push then jump on."

"Ready?" he asked, once Joy was on the cart as well.

"Ready... set... go-cart!" Joy yelled.

Kimani straightened the sail and held on tight. "Push!"

"Doubloon!" DaVinci called.

Daniel leaned into the cart with all his strength. At first, it barely moved. He shoved it one foot, then two feet. Then the wind caught the painting and the wheels started rolling on their own.

Across the sand. Across a hump of beach grass.

Down the dune, picking up speed!

Daniel ran behind it, whooping with excitement, then leaped on board.

Chapter 9

"It's working!" Kimani shouted. "We're sailing!"

"We are unstoppable!" Joy bellowed, raising her arms as the cart rumbled down the dune. "We cannot be stopped!"

Then the cart rolled halfway up the next dune... and stopped.

"Oh, c'mon," Joy said, stomping on the pallet. "Didn't you hear what I just said?"

"I figured this might happen," Kimani said.

"You did?" Daniel asked.

"Yeah, there's probably an equation that tells you how

big a sail you need for what size vehicle, but…"

"It's not in your notebook?"

Kimani shook her head. "Unfortunately not."

"So we need a bigger painting?" Joy asked.

"We need a bigger painting," Kimani agreed. "And a way to steer. I don't *think* we can build a rudder…"

"Can't we just dangle our feet over the side?" Joy asked her. "If we want to turn or stop, we can drag our sneakers in the sand."

"That'll probably work," Kimani said, though she sounded a little disappointed.

"You totally wanted to build a rudder," Daniel teased her as the two of them hiked back to the cave, leaving Joy to untie the canvas from the mast.

"Maybe a little," Kimani admitted.

The bigger painting was waaaay bigger. Daniel broke off the frame's side pieces again, but even with two of them holding it, the wind almost tore it from their hands. Still, they managed to haul it over the dune to the cart and slide it into place on the mast.

But after all their work, Joy made a face. "The bigger sail is better, but look—the mast is barely attached to the pallet, just tied at the bottom. A strong wind could knock the whole cart over."

"Can we brace it?" Daniel asked.

"We don't need to," Joy said. "The answer, as always, is more knots."

She looped rope around the top of the mast, then tied it tightly to one side of the pallet. She did the same on the other three sides so that one rope connected the top of the mast to each side of the cart.

"Pretty!" DaVinci squawked.

"It could be prettier," Joy said. "If we added seashells and ribbons and stuff."

"Let's try this again," Kimani said, holding the top of the painting with one hand and the mast with the other. "I'll keep the sail steady. Joy, scooch over to the left side."

"Aye aye, cap'n!" Joy said. "Consider me scooched!"

"Plank!" DaVinci squawked, standing on the lip of the empty barrel.

"Give us a push," Kimani told Daniel, "then sit on the right. If we need to turn, I'll call out left or—right! Right! Right *now*!"

She shouted that last part because the cart wasn't waiting for Daniel's push. When the wind strengthened, the big painting rippled, the mast bent—and the cart zoomed off!

DaVinci rocketed skyward like a blue-and-yellow streak. "Avast!"

Daniel ran three steps then leaped on board.

The cart jounced and shuddered and knocked Daniel to his knees. He grabbed onto the side with one hand—and onto Kimani's ankle with the other. After he caught his balance, he crawled to the right side of the pallet, the wind cooling the sweat on his face.

The cart picked up speed, racing down a ditch between sandy ridges, the wheels pressing ruts in the beach... then it raced up another dune.

"*Now* we're unstoppable!" Joy cried.

"Stop saying that!" Daniel shouted at her.

"Left!" Kimani called.

Joy stomped downward, her sneaker dragging through the sand, and the cart shifted—barely, the slightest bit—to the left.

"More left!" Kimani said, and turned the painting to catch the wind at a different angle.

The beach blurred past. The cart rattled over the top of a sandy mound, shaking wildly. It felt to Daniel like they'd launched into the air then pounded back down on the other side of the mound, though he knew that was impossible.

To the left, a stream trickled between two dunes. The sail caught the wind and the cart veered to the right, rattling along until—

"Slow down, slow down!" Kimani yelled. "Left *and* right!"

Daniel dug his sneaker in the sand.

"Both of you," Kimani shouted. "Harder, harder!"

The cart slowed a little but suddenly the beach tilted, like the world was turning upside down.

"Abandon ship!" Kimani bellowed.

Chapter 10

Daniel didn't know what was going on, but he didn't waste time asking. He jumped overboard and hit the ground hard—then Joy landed on him even harder.

He groaned. "How do you always do that? You were on the other side of the cart!"

"What happened?" Joy called to Kimani as she crawled off Daniel.

"We were tilting," Kimani said. She was sitting on her butt ten feet away. "About to topple over."

Daniel turned his head and saw that the cart had

slammed to a stop and fallen to one side in the sand.

"This is taking way too long," he groaned.

"The poem didn't say we need to rush," Joy told him.

"It said 'sail to my tower soon, or else!'" he said.

"Oh, that's true."

"And I don't want to miss the captain again." He brushed sand from his shirt and asked Kimani, "Why did the cart fall over?"

"I'm not sure," she said. "Maybe the sail was too high on the mast?"

He thought about the boats he'd seen—and the sketches in the cave. "I think most sails come down low, almost to a ship's deck."

"Yeah, and sails are usually wider at the bottom."

Daniel rolled onto his belly on the beach. "I wonder why."

"Maybe something to do with the center of gravity?" Kimani said.

"What's that?" Joy asked her.

"I'm not exactly sure. But I know a pyramid has a really

low center of gravity, so you can't knock one over. A water bottle has a higher center of gravity, so if you push one, it'll fall easily."

"Joy landed in the center of *my* gravity," Daniel grumbled, eyeing a T-shaped twig stuck in the sand a few inches from his face

"So maybe if we lower the sail," Kimani said, "the wind power will push the cart closer to its low center of gravity and move us forward instead of toppling us over."

"What if we *want* to topple over?" Joy asked.

"We don't, Joy," Daniel said, and the gray twig he'd been eyeing suddenly flapped its wings!

It wasn't a twig—it was an insect.

"Whoa!" he said, and the insect stopped moving and looked like a twig again. "Hey, check this out!"

Joy squatted beside him. "Dead grass? Are you sure I didn't land on your head?"

"Look closer," he said.

"It has legs," Kimani said.

When Daniel blew at it, the twig-insect flapped its
wings—then took off flying and vanished somewhere
between the rolling beach and the blue tropical sky.

"A moth!" Kimani said.

"So cool," Daniel said.

Kimani gazed across the beach. "I wonder how much
life there is out here that we don't even notice."

"What I wonder," Daniel said, "is if there's anything to

eat out here that we haven't noticed."

"There's a whole feast at the tower," Joy told him.

"You think?"

"Of course!" she said, like it was obvious. "Who ever heard of a tower without a feast?"

He blinked at her. Even for Joy, that didn't make much sense.

"C'mon," Joy said. "Let's get moving."

"Avast, matey!" DaVinci squawked, landing on Daniel's shoulder. "Pretty!"

"You're pretty too," Daniel told the parrot before settling him on the small barrel so he wasn't in the way.

Kimani and Joy lowered the painting-sail down the bamboo mast while Daniel kept the cart's wheels from moving, then all three of them hopped aboard. The breeze was gentler, so they didn't move much at first—but soon they were jouncing along the beach again, this time more smoothly.

Daniel sat on the right of the cart with his legs dangling over the side, daydreaming that he was on a real ship. The sea air smelled fresh and DaVinci cooed on his shoulder. The surf crashed against the beach and the ship deck swayed beneath him—well, the pallet shook like maracas, but he ignored that, pretending that the rise and fall of the dunes was the rise and fall of the waves.

"Right," Kimani called, standing at the mast. "Right. A little left..."

The sun warmed Daniel's face. He watched Kimani for a minute, and she glanced away from the front to flash a smile at him. He returned her smile, then looked at the passing dunes, which were now spotted with bushes and shrubs. Joy started singing a song that he barely heard over the creaking, squeaking, and rattling of the cart.

"Right, right," Kimani said, swiveling the sail a few inches. "We're halfway there. The dunes are getting steeper, though. Left! Watch it, we're heading into stormy seas!"

Daniel's smile widened. Apparently he wasn't the only one daydreaming about being on a ship. "Aye, aye," he said.

"Matey!" DaVinci said, and flew in circles around the cart before landing on top of the mast. "Crow's nest! Crow's nest!"

"Hold on!" Kimani said as they neared a steep sandy slope. "This is going to get bumpy!"

The cart tilted backward to climb up the slope, then pointed nose-down after they passed the top and started down the other side—like a rollercoaster about to crash!

"Aaaaaaah!" Daniel screamed.

"Hang on!" Kimani screamed.

"Wheeee!" Joy screamed.

Chapter 11

The cart zoomed down and plunged to the bottom of the slope. The mast creaked and a pallet slat cracked. The cart tilted waaaaaay to the right and the two left-side wheels rose up into the air.

Daniel threw himself backward onto the left side to keep the cart from tipping—and a second later, the front tilted up again as the cart began climbing the next sandy hill.

"Slower, slower!" Kimani said, twisting the sail sideways so it wasn't catching the wind. "Stop!"

Daniel jammed his sneaker to the ground. Little clumps

of grass whipped his ankle. Sand blew everywhere, in his eyes, in his mouth—a sandstorm surrounded him.

The cart tilted, tilted... then rolled to a halt between two dunes, which blocked the wind a little.

"Why'd we stop?" Joy asked breathlessly.

"Because we were about to crash?" Daniel suggested.

"Well, that," Kimani said, "plus I had an idea."

"You had an idea right then? In the middle of all... *that*?"

Kimani nodded. "Yeah, I thought of a way to—"

"Wait a second!" Joy said. "I just realized something huge! This isn't a go-cart at all—it's a *blow*-cart."

Daniel eyed her. "That's huge?"

"Yes! And I also realized what the oozy-squoozy traps are."

"The sands that trap and ooze?" Kimani asked.

Joy nodded. "The closer we get to the tower, the more of those streams between the dunes there are, so the sand is getting all wet and trappy. If we sail into them, we'll get stuck in the mud."

"Yeah, I saw those too," Kimani told her. "That's what

I've been guiding us around."

"Oh, I thought you were just trying to catch the wind," Joy said.

"Yeah," Daniel said. "And to avoid any super-steep dunes."

Joy squinted at Kimani. "You knew about the sand, but you still didn't know we built a *blow*cart!"

"Very true," Kimani said.

"So what's your idea?" Daniel asked her.

Kimani said, "Well, we've almost tipped over like five times. We need to widen the base of the cart to lower the center of gravity."

"You want to widen the cart?" Daniel frowned. "But we don't have more pallets."

"So instead, we'll extend the wheels out to the sides."

"Huh?"

"Like this," Kimani said, and drew a sketch in her notebook.

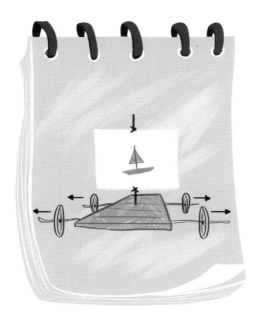

He looked at the drawing. "Oh, slide the wheels along the extra bamboo that's poking out the sides! To make the wheels stick out farther."

"Which *should* keep us from tipping," Kimani said.

While Joy started untying the knots that kept the wheels in place, Daniel climbed a dune to have a look at the streams that made the sandy traps.

But the first thing he noticed was the tower—which was much closer now. Yellow flowers covered the hill that the tower stood on, but from his angle he couldn't see the front door, which was hidden by a bunch of white boulders. Meadows peeked from beyond the tower—and he thought he heard the chittering of monkeys from the rainforest.

"Where are the oozy traps?" he asked DaVinci when the parrot landed on his shoulder.

"Matey!"

"Thanks," Daniel said. "That helps."

"Pretty parrot!" DaVinci told him, and a flash of light glinted between two sandy dunes.

It was sunlight reflecting off a stream that flowed between the dunes. And streams meant water—which meant mud that could trap the cart's wheels.

"I'm glad Kimani's steering," Daniel said.

DaVinci squawked, "Way!"

"That's what I want to know," Kimani said, climbing up the dune beside Daniel.

"Huh?"

"Which way should we go," she explained. "Isn't that what you were saying?"

"Oh. Yeah. Well, my big idea is 'aim for the tower.'"

She nudged him. "I mean, which way should we go to avoid getting bogged down in those oozy mud traps. We need to plot a safe path through."

"It's like a maze," Daniel said, shading his eyes to see better. "Oh! Do you see that dune just before the tower hill? The one covered with grass and flowers? When the wind blows, it looks like it's wobbling!"

"It's waterlogged from all the streams at the bottom." She tugged at her ponytail. "That's a lot of traps to dodge."

"You'll find a way between them," Daniel told her.

From behind them, Joy yelled, "I finished untying! Come help with the wheels! We don't want to be late for the feast."

Daniel and Kimani trotted back together. "There better be a feast," Daniel told Joy. "This blowcarting is hungry work."

"You're always hungry," Joy said.

"I wouldn't be if someone hadn't knocked my doughnut to the ground."

"It wasn't my fault," she said. "It had a really bad center of gravity."

Daniel made a face at her, then he and Kimani lifted the pallet while Joy slid the wheels, one at a time, farther out along the bamboo axle.

"There," Kimani said, when they finished. "That'll definitely make the base of the cart wider and more stable."

While Joy started tying knots on the axles to keep the wheels in place, Daniel grabbed a handful of sand and let it pour through his fingers. It felt different here. Rougher and heavier. And spiky bushes grew in this area, while a few high stalks of grass bent in the wind.

"Looking for camouflaged twig moths?" Kimani asked, sitting beside him.

"I am now," he said.

"You won't see them," Joy told him, walking over. "They're camouflaged."

"That doesn't make them invisible," Daniel said, just as a cricket leaped in front of him from a bush. "Whoa! Neat."

"It's camouflaged too, a little," Kimani said. "Sort of sandy-colored."

"It's pretty," Daniel said.

"Now you sound like DaVinci," Kimani told him.

"DaVinci would eat it," Joy said.

Kimani said, "Nobody's going to eat it!"

There was a blur of motion beside the cricket and a small hole opened in the sand. With a flash of forelegs, a creature darted from the hole, grabbed the cricket, then dragged it back into the hole and vanished.

Even the hole disappeared!

Chapter 12

Daniel and Kimani yelped and scooted backward, but there was nothing there. Just a blank stretch of sand, like they'd imagined the whole thing.

Except Joy said, "A spider! So cool!"

"You like spiders?" Kimani asked her.

"I love them."

Kimani squinted at her. "So you're afraid of big, sweet, huggable snakes, but you love *spiders*?"

"Spiders are furry," Joy explained.

"They have eight legs!" Kimani said.

Joy sighed longingly. "I wish I had eight legs."

"Whoa, whoa," Daniel said. "Hold up. What just happened?!"

"A spider ate a cricket," Joy explained.

"But where'd the spider come from?" he asked. "And more important—where'd it *go*?"

"It's still there," Joy told him. "Underground. Waiting. That must've been a trapdoor spider. They dig burrows, then build roofs of dirt and leaves with little silken hinges."

"Hinges?" Kimani said, brightening. "Really?"

"Yup. And when something tasty comes close…" Joy made fangs with her fingers and snapped at Daniel. "Spider feast!"

Kimani squinched up her face. "That's enough to make me lose my appetite."

"Me too," Daniel said.

"You never lose your appetite," Joy told him.

"That is so…" He thought for a second. "…true!"

Joy grinned. "So let's get moving. We're almost there."

"Yeah," Daniel said. "And we need to get there 'soon,' after all."

After they loaded the barrels back onto the cart, Joy took her place on the left side while Kimani stood at the mast, steadying the sail—and turning it when she needed.

DaVinci returned to his "crow's nest" atop the bamboo mast, squawking, "Pretty!" and "Matey" and "DaVinci!"

Then Daniel shoved the cart uphill—which was pretty easy with the help of wind power pushing on the sail. Kimani told him when to jump onto the pallet, and he scooted into place a second before the cart crested another dune.

A strong ocean breeze caught the sail and sent the cart speeding along the beach. The wheels bumped over sandy ridges and crashed through brittle bushes.

Kimani yelled, "Left, left—slower—great!" and wrestled the sail first in one direction then in the other.

This time everything felt way steadier.

"Wow," Daniel said. "Spreading the wheels out really worked."

"Right!" Kimani said.

Daniel nodded in agreement. "Right!"

"No, *turn* right, *turn right*!"

He dragged his sneaker in the sand and Kimani twisted the sail, and the cart shifted a teensy bit to the right.

Which must've been enough, because Kimani yelled, "Perfect!"

The tower loomed higher every time Daniel checked. He could see the circular stone building with vines and windows and a big wooden door at the bottom. The grassy hill leading up to it wasn't nearly as steep as he'd thought, not like the side they had seen from the rainforest during their last adventure.

White boulders dotted leafy hedges and sandy paths... including one path that led from the tower straight to the beach.

Daniel almost shouted in triumph, but then he saw another glimmer of sunlight. Streams and puddles dotted the dunes at the base of the hill!

He called out a warning, and Kimani said, "I see it!"

The breeze ruffled Daniel's hair and plucked at his shirt. The wide-base cart swept across the beach, dodging the muddy traps as Kimani steered them safely past.

Daniel almost laughed—then he saw that some dunes were so waterlogged, like Kimani had said, that they wobbled and shook like massive mud pies. He groaned to himself. There was no way they'd miss those. They *always* bumped into every obstacle!

Joy noticed the bizarre wobbly dunes and yelled, "Pudding!"

"If a wheel gets stuck in one of those," Daniel shouted, "we'll never get free."

"I have a plan!" Kimani yelled, staring straight ahead.

"What's that?" he asked.

"'Don't get stuck in the pudding!'" she called with wild excitement in her voice.

She sounded a little like Joy, which made Daniel nervous. So he opened his mouth to tell her to be careful, but instead heard himself yell: "We're unstoppable! We cannot be stopped!"

"Full speed ahead!" DaVinci squawked, swooping down to fly beside them.

The cart raced into the final stretch of dunes, squeaking and slamming and shaking toward the base of the hill, which rose in front of them... just past a bunch of wobbly dunes and a reedy pond.

"Faster, faster!" Joy yelled. "Faster!"

"Right, right!" Kimani shouted.

Daniel dug his heel into the sand. "Woohoo!"

"Go go!" Joy called.

"Ahoy!" DaVinci squawked.

"Slower!" Kimani screamed.

THUNK! the cart said, and slammed to a stop.

Chapter 13

The front right wheel slammed into a half-buried rock.

Daniel clung to the side of the pallet to keep from getting thrown off. The cart spun sideways and started tipping over.

Kimani flew into the sand with an "Oof!"

The barrels rolled off the pallet and Daniel's side of the cart scraped the ground while the other side rose higher. Then everything stopped except for one wheel, spinning in the air.

"Is everyone okay?" Daniel called.

"Yeah, but the mast broke," Kimani said.

"That doesn't matter!" Joy popped up from the other side of the pallet. "We're here!"

Daniel stood and saw that the hill started about ten feet from them. The wide path climbed toward the tower, sandy at the bottom but carpeted with flowers toward the top. It led straight uphill between the scattered white boulders and the wildflower-speckled grass.

The tower door gleamed in the sun, warm and welcoming. And on the breeze, the scent of seaweed and sand dunes mixed with...

"Do you smell that?" he asked, sniffing.

"My nose is full of sand," Kimani said, stretching her hand out to Daniel.

He pulled her to her feet. "It smells sweet. Like dessert."

"Like a whole feast," Joy said, getting to her feet.

"We still need to drag the barrels up this hill," Kimani said.

"At least it's not that far now," Daniel said. "Not half as far as a football field."

"Yeah, and we can push the cart up the last hill without the sail."

"That sounds—"

"Ooh!" Joy said, hopping around. "Ooh! Ooh!"

Daniel peered at her. "What?"

"Look!" She pointed uphill. "We have very own greeters!"

Dark shapes scurried across the hillside and leaped onto the boulders around the flowery path. The clusters of small furry creatures gathered on top of the boulders looked like—

"Monkeys," Daniel said.

"They probably smelled dessert too," Kimani said.

Daniel nodded. "Yeah, and they don't like to share. I hope Captain Wei doesn't let them in her tower."

"Because you don't like to share either," Joy said.

"Because *someone* threw my doughnut on the ground!"

"Will you let go of that missing doughnut already?" Kimani said to Daniel, then turned to Joy. "And will you untie the mast? To make the pushing easier? We'll reload the barrels."

Daniel eyed the monkeys as he hefted the glue barrel back onto the cart. He didn't trust monkeys, not since they'd threatened him, Joy, and Kimani back in rainforest. Still, the monkeys were just milling around on the boulders now. Grooming each other, chomping on fruit, staying calm and quiet.

"Maybe they *are* greeters," he said.

"Ahoy!" DaVinci called, swooping past Daniel.

"Exactly," Daniel said. "They're just here to say ahoy."

DaVinci landed beside a pond that rippled below a nearby dune. He marched across the shore, which glittered with salt crystals.

"Walk the plank!" he called. With every step, a sheet of crusty salt cracked under his feet. "Walk the plank!"

"Be nice," Kimani told DaVinci. "The monkeys can stick around as long as they don't bother us."

DaVinci started to dunk his beak into the water and Daniel shouted, "Don't drink that! It's saltwater!"

"Yo ho ho!" DaVinci called back.

"Yeah, I'm thirsty too," Daniel told him. "I hope there's juice at this feast."

He shoved the barrels back onto the middle of the cart and Kimani said, "Let's get pushing."

"Aye, aye, captain," Joy told her.

Kimani looked pleased and embarrassed at the same time. "Would you stop calling me that?"

"Yeah, Joy," Daniel said, before saluting Kimani.

Kimani smacked his arm, and he grinned as he grabbed the back of the cart. The girls got into position on either side of him, then they all started pushing.

The cart bumped along the sandy section of the path. The pallet trembled in Daniel's hands. The sea breeze swept across the beach behind him. The grass in the meadow beyond the tower fluttered, and the rainforest leaves shimmered and shook.

Joy starting chanting in time with her steps: "Left, right, left, right! I left my doughnut on the train and don't have dessert *left*!"

Daniel snorted, but kept his head and down and pushed. His hands started aching a little—but in a good way. They were almost there.

"Left, right, left, right," Joy chanted as she pushed. "I crashed my blowcart into a hill without any flotsam *left*!"

Kimani laughed. "What does that even mean?"

DaVinci swooped past Daniel, zoomed a few inches above the barrels, then shot ahead and landed on that broad stone step in front of the tower's door. So close!

Daniel smiled as the cart rolled onto the flowery section of the path. The bright yellow blossoms reminded him of a welcome mat.

He pushed harder in excitement, and the cart rumbled into the shadow of a boulder. The wheels squeaked, the wind blew, Joy chanted—

And the monkeys SCREAMED, leaping down from the boulder and landing on the path in front of them.

Chapter 14

The path ahead looked like a monkey avalanche, an angry churning pile of gleaming eyes and hairy arms and grasping hands.

Joy yelled, "Hey! Get out of our way!"

Two monkeys in front bared their teeth—and one of them flung sand at them.

"Stupid monkeys," Daniel muttered.

"I guess they really don't want to share," Kimani said.

"Greedy monkeys," Daniel muttered.

"Go away!" Joy yelled. "Shoo! Start marching! You

left your dinner in the rainforest and don't have any monkeyfruit *left*!"

Even the angriest monkeys looked a little confused by that. They stared for a baffled second before screaming louder.

"Let's back up," Kimani said. "Maybe there's another way in."

"I hope it's a quick one," Daniel said, helping her pull the cart backward. "I bet we're running out of time. We never get to stay very long."

The monkeys settled down the minute they backed off. The troop climbed back up on the boulders and lounged around peacefully, like they'd never flung a single handful of sand.

"I'll check this way," Daniel said, after they parked the cart against a hedge to keep it from rolling downhill.

He stepped off the path to look at the side of the tower. The groundcover changed from sand to bouncy grass and tangles of wildflowers.

What if there wasn't another entrance? Daniel worried. How would they get in? Maybe they could climb through a window? Except even the lowest windows were way too high. Still, if they built a ladder or—

"Daniel, freeze!" Joy yelled.

He stopped. "What?"

"The ground is moving!"

When he looked down, he felt seasick. The carpet of wildflowers was wobbling around him. It wasn't bouncy grass—it was waterlogged sand shaking under his sneakers.

He dashed back toward the path. Every time he took another step, the ground wobbled and his footprint filled with water.

Still, he managed to reach the solid path and lunge to safety without being trapped by the hillside.

"Are you okay?" Kimani asked.

"Y-yeah," he said, and his voice only shook a little. "I guess we learned one thing."

Kimani nodded. "There isn't another way in."

"At least not in time," Daniel said.

"There has to be *some* way in," Joy said.

"Way!" DaVinci squawked from the stone step at the tower doorway.

"Great idea," Joy called to him. "But we can't fly over the monkeys like you, DaVinci!"

"I'd settle for being a twig moth," Daniel said.

"*I'd* settle for being a trapdoor spider," Joy said.

"How would that help?"

"Two words," she said. "All-you-can-eat-cricket buffet!"

"That's like ten words. And also, gross."

"That's it!" Kimani blurted. "That's how we get in!"

Daniel eyed her suspiciously. "Crickets?"

"Spiders!" Joy said. "We'll burrow beneath the monkeys."

"Would you two hush?" Kimani said. "What do crickets, trapdoor spiders, and twig moths all have in common?"

Daniel knew that one. "Too many legs!"

"No—well, yes, but what else?"

"Camouflage," Joy said.

"That's right," Kimani said. "We're going to turn ourselves invisible."

Chapter 15

"**C**amouflage!" Daniel repeated. "Of course."

Joy's eyes shone with glee. "We'll dress up as monkeys!"

"Uh, no," Kimani told her. "We'll use the cart like that spider uses its trapdoor. We'll pile sand and flowers on top, then crawl underneath and—"

"We'll push it along without the monkeys seeing us!" Daniel said. "That's beyond genius. That's super-genius."

"Let's go get the sail," Kimani told Daniel. "Otherwise the sand will fall through the cracks between the pallet slats."

"So we'll lay the painting—I mean, the sail—on the cart with sand on top?"

"Exactly." Kimani started downhill to where they'd left the painting. "And meanwhile, Joy can collect other stuff for camouflage."

"We need to hurry," Daniel said, trotting after Kimani. "We don't have much time."

"You don't know that for sure," Joy called after him as she started gathering flowers. "Maybe this time we have days and days to achieve our mission!"

"Days and days isn't 'soon,'" he called back. "And I don't want to run out of time and miss something important."

"Like food!" she shouted, though he barely heard her over the wind rising again.

Still, he yelled, "I don't want to miss *Captain Wei*!"

Bringing the painting back took no time at all compared to pushing the cart uphill. Then he and Kimani laid it on the pallet, added more sand, and put the barrels on top.

Joy arranged lots of flowers and chunks of grass to hide

the barrels—and to make the whole cart look more like a part of the path.

"There we go," she said, stepping back to admire the camouflaged cart.

"Looks good," Daniel said.

"Let's see if it fools the monkeys," Kimani said. "If we…"

She trailed off when the strengthening wind started blowing across the cart.

At first, just a few blades of grass flew away.

Then a few flowers.

Then Joy threw herself onto the cart to keep everything in place, but a powerful gust of wind swept all her camouflage to the ground.

"I guess wind power is the enemy now," Daniel said with a sigh, watching the flowers tumble away.

"My poor burrow!" Joy groaned.

He blinked at her. "Your *burrow*?"

"We were going to be trapdoor spiders," she said. "Hiding under the cart."

"A three-headed spider," he said. "At least we would've had the right number of legs."

"If you count DaVinci," Kimani added.

"Maybe we can glue the flowers to the painting?" Joy asked, kneeling on the cart and frowning at the barrels.

Daniel sniffed the air. "I'm sure I can smell fruit punch."

"I don't think that'll work," Kimani told Joy. "This is white glue. It'll take too long to harden."

"Yeah," Joy agreed. "And it'd look weird too."

"I wonder if there's pizza," Daniel said.

Kimani nodded to Joy. "We want the cart to look as much like these waterlogged dunes as possible. The better the camouflage, the better our chances."

"I've heard of forest camo and desert camo," Daniel said. "But never wobbly-dune camo."

Kimani frowned thoughtfully. "Hmm. I have an idea, but we don't have the ingredients."

"Ingredients?" Joy asked. "Like for cooking?"

"I hope so," Daniel said. "I'm starving."

Kimani ignored them both. "We have plenty of glue, but there's no borax."

"What's borax?" Joy asked.

"Yo ho ho!" DaVinci called from the tower.

Daniel peered toward him. "You're not drinking saltwater again, are you?"

"*Salt*water..." Kimani said, then broke into a smile. "No way."

"Way!" DaVinci squawked.

"What?" Daniel asked.

Kimani laughed. "It can't be! Can it? We have glue, and if that's borax... what else do we need?"

"An explanation?" Daniel said.

"Water!" Kimani pointed at the pond where DaVinci had been marching around. "Do you see those crystals on the shore?"

"You mean the crusty stuff?" Daniel asked.

Kimani nodded hard. "That's got to be borax."

"Uh, what's that?"

"A kind of salt that collects in evaporated lakes. And there's no way that—"

"Way!" DaVinci interrupted.

"—that Captain Wei didn't provide borax along with the glue," Kimani continued.

"I still don't know what borax is," Daniel told her. "Or why we need it."

"It's one of the key ingredients," Kimani said.

He squinted at her. "For *what*?"

"Our next creation!" she said. "Then we'll just add sand and flowers and grass. Perfect, perfect, perfect!"

"Perfect!" Joy agreed.

"What is?" Daniel asked her, while Kimani rummaged in her backpack.

"I have no idea," Joy admitted. "She'll probably tell us in a second."

Kimani pulled out her notebook and said, "Slime!"

"Sheesh," Joy told her. "You don't have to call us names."

Chapter 16

"**N**ot *you*!" Kimani said. "What I mean is, we have all the ingredients to make slime! We can use slime to camouflage the cart exactly like the wobbly hillside—and nothing will blow away!"

"Slime like... slime?" Daniel asked. "Like the goopy stuff you play with?"

"Exactly, and we've got enough raw material to make loads." Kimani flipped another page in her notebook. "Let's see, one part white glue to one part water..."

"What does that mean?" Daniel asked.

"The same amount of each," Kimani explained. "So we'll use all the glue in this barrel, then fill the same barrel from the pond to get the same amount of water."

"And then the flowers and stuff?" Joy asked.

"Well, first we need to make sure we have the right amount of borax." Kimani chewed her lip as she read from her notebook. "Hm, I guess it's already dissolved in the pond, so we can't really adjust the amount."

"I still don't know what borax is," Daniel told her, "other than a kind of salt."

"It's the activator that turns slime from a gloppy mess to a beautiful blob," Kimani explained.

"An activator? That sounds like Joy."

"I'd rather be an activator than a gloppy mess," Joy said.

"After we make our slime and cover the cart with it, we'll add the decorations," Kimani said. "And then we'll have our camouflage."

"So this is why we needed the barrels," Joy said as she began to put together the clues in the note from Captain Wei in her mind. "To make sure we brought the glue. I was wondering about that."

"I thought it was just to make the challenge harder," Daniel admitted.

Joy grinned. "I think Captain Wei likes surprises."

"We need something to stir with," Kimani said, looking around.

"I'll grab a piece of the broken mast," Daniel said, and headed toward the bamboo pole they'd left downhill. Then he turned back and asked Kimani, "You have the recipe for slime in your notebook?"

"Maybe," Kimani said.

"How about the recipe for chocolate-glazed doughnuts?"

"Go get the bamboo!" she yelled, and he ran off smiling.

* * *

By the time Daniel returned, Kimani had started making the slime in the empty barrel because it was the biggest. She and

Joy had already poured in the glue, so he and Kimani used the now empty glue barrel to add an equal amount of water.

"I hope that really is borax," Kimani said as they poured.

"What if it's not?" Daniel asked.

"Then we'll end up with glue soup."

Daniel made a face. "I'm not *that* hungry."

Joy stirred the mixture with the broken mast piece, and

in seconds the glue began to turn into a thick, gloopy slime.

"Borax confirmed," Kimani said, clapping her hands.

"That is one beautiful blob," Daniel said.

Joy added sand to the barrel, then they poured the sandy slime onto the painting. It oozed to the sides until it covered the whole thing. Joy carefully poked tufts of grass and arrangements of flowers into the slime, camouflaging

the cart so it would blend in with the rest of the hill.

Suddenly a stiff breeze blew in off the ocean.

Daniel held his breath. On the slime-covered cart, the stalks of grass shivered and the flower petals fluttered—but everything stayed in place.

Even better, the whole thing wobbled slightly, exactly like the waterlogged dunes.

"That's amazing!" Kimani told Joy.

"You really are a trapdoor spider," Daniel said.

Joy flushed happily and said, "Okay, let's get burrowing."

Tugging and shoving, they aimed the cart toward the wooden door, beyond the boulders and the monkeys. Then they squirmed beneath the pallet, each holding a piece of rope that Joy had used to steady the mast. Daniel grabbed the rope tied to the rear and wrapped it around his right hand while the girls grabbed the ropes tied to the sides. Hidden under the camouflaged cart, they started crawling to the tower.

The ropes they were holding pulled the cart along with

them in little jerky motions. Moving slowly. Staying quiet. Letting the monkeys get used to this pretty patch of dune that just happened to have wheels sticking out of it.

The jerkiness smoothed out... but Joy's right foot kicked sand into Daniel's face.

Then Kimani's left foot kicked sand into Daniel's face.

Then the path turned to flowers beneath him, and nobody kicked sand in his face.

When Daniel peeked around Joy, the tower was so close that he could make out the design carved into the wooden door: a circle filled with colored stars.

So close!

The rope tugged against his hand, the wheels rolled... and the shadow of a boulder dimmed the sunlight. Daniel gritted his teeth, waiting for the monkeys to leap down at them.

Nothing happened, though, as the cart squeaked closer to the tower.

Fifty feet away. Forty feet away.

They rolled past one boulder, and the monkeys didn't leap down on them. Daniel felt a spark of excitement. It was working! They were totally invisible.

They got thirty feet from the tower, and the monkeys still didn't have a clue. They were better camouflaged than a twig moth in a... in a pile of *other* twig moths!

Except when they rolled past the last boulder, the monkeys started chattering in alarm. Monkey feet slapped against stone as they ran back and forth.

"Oh no," Daniel whispered.

The cart was squeaking way too loudly. *Squeak, rattle, creak. Clatter, squeal, squeal.* There was no way the monkeys could miss all that noise.

He braced for another avalanche of fangs to pour down from the boulder just behind them... but the next thing he heard was a voice squawking, "Pretty parrot! Swab the deck! Avast, DaVinci! You're pretty! Abaft the beam! Hard to port!"

Ha! DaVinci was chattering nonstop, distracting the

monkeys! And making so much noise that they couldn't hear the rattling and squeaking cart.

"Good parrot," Daniel whispered.

He focused on the ache of the rope in his hand, the warmth of the flowery grass on his knees, and the hope blossoming in his heart. The tower was right there and—

Scrape!

One of the axles snagged on a boulder.

Daniel winced, but the noise wasn't their biggest problem. No, their biggest problem was that a wheel *fell off the cart.* For a frozen second, he just stared at it: a dented wooden wheel lying on the flowery ground.

Then the cart tipped onto one corner, which gave Daniel a clear view of the monkeys on the boulder.

And which gave *them* a clear view of *him.*

At first, they mostly seemed baffled. Like they were wondering how a section of the flowery path had laid a Daniel-shaped egg.

Then a big monkey leaped down from the boulder and

bared his teeth.

"Aw, c'mon," Joy called to him. "Don't be like that."

Then a bunch of other monkeys jumped down and joined the big one, pacing and shrieking and smacking the ground.

"New plan," Kimani said. *"Run for it!"*

"Way!" DaVinci squawked, and the monkeys charged.

Chapter 17

Daniel scrambled out from under the tilted cart—at least he tried to, but his head banged the pallet and he smacked his elbow while untangling the rope from around his hand.

Joy sprang to her feet in front of him. "Stop messing around!"

"I'm too big!" he said.

"Being short rules!" she said, and grabbed his arm to pull him out from under the cart.

"C'mon, c'mon!" Kimani said, rolling the loose wheel

toward the monkeys.

"Eeeeeeeee!" the monkeys screamed, dodging the wheel and rampaging closer. "Oooeeeee!"

Kimani raced for the tower and Daniel followed, trying to drag Joy along by her hand.

But Joy shook free and yelled at Kimani, "*That's* not how you throw things at monkeys. *This* is how you throw things at monkeys!"

Then she hurled a handful of slime at them and took off past Daniel, laughing like a hyena.

The monkeys shrieked even louder. Daniel saw what looked like a hundred gleaming fangs and enraged faces as he sprinted desperately away—

But only for like five steps, because the tower was *right there*.

His sneakers slapped against the stone step in front of

the closed door... and the monkeys stopped chasing him. They stopped shrieking too. They just wandered off toward the rainforest like they didn't even care.

"Did you see that?" Joy said. "I chased them off."

"I think they don't get too close to the tower," Kimani said.

"Yeah," Joy said. "Because they're afraid of getting slimed."

Kimani grabbed the big brass doorknob. "Okay. Ready to go inside?"

"Always," Joy said.

"No," Daniel said.

Kimani blinked at him. "Why not?"

"It can't be this easy," he said.

"Easy?" Kimani laughed. "Daniel, we had to build a blowcart with stuff from a cave and sneak past vicious monkeys using slime camouflage!"

"Oh. That's true."

"And avoid the wobbly traps," Joy said. "And figure out how to fix the sails."

Daniel considered. "You don't think one more thing's going to jump out at us?"

"Avast, matey!" DaVinci squawked, landing on Daniel's shoulder. "Way! Way!"

"I'm pretty sure that means DaVinci thinks it's okay," Joy said.

"Walk the plank!" DaVinci said.

"So *now* are we all ready?" Kimani said.

"Still always," Joy said.

"Okay." Daniel took a deep breath. "Ready."

Kimani pulled the door open.

Chapter 18

Cool air wafted around Daniel's face from inside the tower. The door opened into a big, round room. A circular staircase hugged the stone walls, spiraling upward, leading toward the high ceiling.

The really, *really* high ceiling.

Daylight streamed from the windows and shone on, well, nothing. Because the room was totally empty.

"Hello?" Joy shouted, her voice echoing upward. "Captain Wei? We're here!"

"I hope we're not too late," Daniel said when there was

no answer.

"The tower's shaped like a lighthouse," Kimani said. "I bet she's waiting for us at the top."

"Where is she?" Daniel asked DaVinci.

"Crow's nest! Crow's nest!" the parrot squawked.

"Told you so," Kimani said.

They climbed the spiral staircase, around and around and around. Daniel passed a window overlooking the sandy beach that stretched to the cliffs with the cave where their adventure began. Around and around, and Kimani paused at a view of the rainforest canopy and the swamp where the anaconda lived. Around even more, until Joy pointed at a big rock off the shore, where they'd built a bridge the first time they were brought to the island.

And finally, they came to a ladder that led up to a door in the ceiling.

"A trapdoor," Joy whispered in wonder.

"That means you go first, spider-girl," Kimani told her.

For once, Joy didn't say anything. She just smiled and

climbed the ladder. Then she threw open the trapdoor and
vanished inside.

When Daniel followed Kimani through, he found
himself in a small circular room that had been divided
in half by a hanging tapestry. The half that Daniel could
see reminded him of a ship captain's cabin. Goblets and
charts and spyglasses cluttered a table. Heavy drapes hung
around a narrow bed in the corner beside a bunch of open

chests—overflowing with velvet cloth and silver coins and, for some reason, brightly colored plastic balls.

Books and maps and magazines stuffed a bookshelf, and dozens of models dangled from strings attached to the ceiling. Models of ships, cars, buildings, and rockets. There were even a few stuffed animals, but Daniel barely noticed those because he was staring at the tower's walls, which were made of glass.

"Like a lighthouse," he said, his voice hushed.

"Or the best burrow ever," Joy said.

He crossed to the glass wall and gazed outside. The beach spread beneath him, the dunes and the streams. The blue sky looked close enough to touch. A flock of birds followed the coastline, all of them tilting and turning at exactly the same time.

"Look at that," Kimani said, pointing out the window.

A dozen other islands dotted the ocean beyond the beach. One rose like a mountain, and another vanished every time a wave rolled past. Some had jungles, some had lakes, and smoke curled from the top of one that looked like a volcano.

"Welcome to my home," a low, musical voice said behind them.

Chapter 19

"Captain Wei!" Joy cried, spinning around. "You're here!"

Daniel turned from the window and saw Captain Wei
step out from behind the tapestry that divided the room.
Instead of a tricorn hat, she was wearing a red bandana
this time—the same color as their headbands! Her black
hair fell around a frilly shirt, and she wore patched pants
and high boots—and dozens of earrings and necklaces and
bracelets.

"What's impressive is that *you're* here," Captain Wei
said. "You did it again."

"We're great at messing up," Daniel explained.

Kimani said, "Daniel!"

"Messing up is a good thing," he told her. "Because we learn and we keep trying."

Captain Wei's laugh sounded like windchimes. "Very true. So much is possible when you work together as a crew."

"Crew!" DaVinci landed on the captain's shoulder. "Pretty crew!"

"Do you remember the second poem you found?" the captain asked as she stroked DaVinci's head.

"Not really," Daniel said. "But I remember you told us there was a 'greater challenge' in store."

"Hmm." Kimani took her notebook out of her backpack. "Let's see..."

"The second poem's about flying through the rainforest without any wings," Joy told her.

"That was the third poem," Kimani said. "We found two that first trip, remember? The first started with 'One path is safe for your brave band,' and then we found a second poem inside the shipwreck."

"Oh, right!" Joy said. "The shipwreck one didn't make much sense."

Kimani had written all the poems down, so she read aloud from her notebook:

> *You'll play the games,*
>
> *You'll face the trials,*
>
> *You'll meet the challenge,*
>
> *Of these magic isles.*
>
> *A team you'll forge,*
>
> *Before you're through,*
>
> *You'll protect the chain,*
>
> *From the fateful spew.*

"What chain?" Joy peered at Captain Wei. "Like a necklace? A magic necklace!"

"It means the *island* chain," Kimani said. "And the

'fateful spew' is... "

"Is what?" Daniel asked.

Kimani peered through the window. "That smoking volcano's going to erupt, isn't it?"

"Yes," Captain Wei said, and her gaze seemed to focus on something far away. "I was stranded here a long time ago, after my armada was lost in a strange storm. The islands chose me as their protector, but I cannot do this alone. I need your help."

"Hold on!" Daniel said. "The volcano? As in—*that* volcano? Right over there? It's erupting?!"

"I told you she likes surprises!" Joy said as she nudged him.

"We're not in danger," Captain Wei assured Daniel. "There's plenty of time. Well, there's *enough* time. That's why you started training already, learning teamwork and problem solving."

"And science," Kimani said with a nod. "And engineering."

"You should teach us magic instead," Joy told Captain Wei.

"You don't need my magic, Joy," Captain Wei said. "You don't need spells or wands. You and your friends already make the magic happen on your own."

"But I don't know any magic," Joy said.

The captain laughed and took her hands. "You engineered a bridge out of triangles so you could walk across the ocean. You overcame the force of friction and flew through the rainforest. You built a perfect pulley system that saved a baby monkey."

"An *ungrateful* baby monkey," Daniel muttered.

"That's magic, Joy," Captain Wei continued. "The more you understand the secrets of science, the art of engineering, and the rules and rhythms of the world around you, the more magic you hold inside you."

Joy wrinkled her nose. "So when we built a blowcart that could travel across the beach, we were making our own magic?"

"Exactly!" The captain spread her arms, which made her bracelets jingle. "And with imagination and teamwork, you spread the magic all around you."

"So what's the next step?" Daniel asked. "Tell us quick before we run out of time,"

"Run out of time?" Captain Wei asked, her eyebrows drawing together quizzically.

"Yeah, before the drums sends us back home. You said we needed to get here soon."

"And you did," Captain Wei told him, reaching for the tapestry that divided the room. "You got here much sooner than I'd expected."

"We did?" he asked.

"Because I slimed the monkeys," Joy said.

"Because Kimani dodged the traps," Daniel said. "And knows about sails."

"Because we all worked together," Kimani said.

"The drums will send you home at sunset, Daniel..." Captain Wei slid the tapestry open. "...but the next step is a feast!"

Buffet tables filled the other half of the room. Mounds

of monkeyfruit surrounded bananas and melons and weird-shaped fruit that Daniel didn't recognize. Bamboo straws poked from the tops of coconuts beside bowls of rock candy and even a few doughnuts.

"Look! There's a chocolate-glazed one," Joy said, grabbing it from a tray.

"Now *that* is my kind of surprise," Daniel said.

After a moment, Joy handed the doughnut to Daniel. "Sorry I dropped your other one."

The scent of fudgy sweetness reminded Daniel of being on the subway platform. Except now he understood that there was magic, even there. The lights shining from the ceilings and the trains zooming through the tunnels had come from someone's imagination. From a whole bunch of people, working together as a team. Brainstorming and building, testing and improving, then retesting and improving again until the problem was solved—and magic happened.

"That's okay," he told Joy. "I wasn't hungry anyway."

Joy and Kimani laughed, and Daniel took a bite.

ARE YOU UP TO THE CHALLENGE?

Hang onto yer headbands, lads and lassies—it's time for your Blowcart Beach challenge! Arrrr ye ready to build a wind-powered pirate ship that can sail the high seas? Every pirate knows that good masts and sails are the keys to a happy voyage, so design them well, me hearties. Then celebrate your sailing success by mixing up a batch of Pirate Treasure Slime, using the recipe in Kimani's notebook plus a few treasure-y mix-ins. Are you ready? Sail on!

THINK LIKE A PIRATE WITH JOY

 **Y**o ho ho, team-mateys! To build a pirate ship, you need to start thinking like a pirate. Let's start by learning more about who pirates are and what they do on their voyages.

A Pirate's Life

Pirates are sea robbers—and pirates still exist! They sail the oceans in search of other boats and seafront villages to steal from. Pirates have been around since ancient times, but during the Golden Age of Pirates (1650–1730), they were everywhere, spread as thickly across the high seas as chocolate frosting on Daniel's favorite doughnut. These seafaring scoundrels would attack ginormous booty-filled boats in search of gold, rubies, pearls, and doubloons (Spanish coins made of gold). Other favorite pirate booty included barrels filled with helpful supplies like food and fresh water.

Shiver me timbers!

Pirates give themselves and their ships tough-sounding names in hopes of striking terror in the hearts of other sailors. One of the most feared pirates was a man in the 1700s called Blackbeard and his ship was the *Queen Anne's Revenge.* When Blackbeard went into battle, he braided pieces of rope into his beard and hair and set them on fire!

Pick Your Pirate Name

Now it's time to pick out your pirate name. Create your tough new title by choosing a first name and a last name from the chart on the next page—or create a unique pirate name of your own. For example, Daniel would definitely be Doughnut-Breath McStinky, and you can call me Coconut Kidd!

Pick a First Name

Anaconda

Coconut

Doughnut-Breath

Piranha

Quicksand

Sharktooth

Shipwreck

Zipline

Pick a Last Name

Doubleloon

Jack

Jones

Kidd

McStinky

Of the Seas

O'Slime

Sparrow

Next, you'll need a terrifying name for the pirate ship you are about to build. The name should be fun but frightening. How about something like Dragon's Breath, Wicked Waves, or Boat of Rattling Bones?

Talk Like A Pirate

The final step to thinking like a pirate is talking like one! Here are a some of my favorite pirate terms:

ahoy – hello

arrrrr – I'm excited

avast ye! – pay attention

blimey – I'm surprised

booty – treasure

heave ho – use your muscles

landlubber – an inexperienced pirate

matey – friend

me hearties – my BFFs

poop deck – the high deck at the back of the ship

scallywag – troublemaker

scurvy dog – scoundrel

sea dog – an experienced pirate

swashbuckling – brave and adventurous

timbers – masts

Now yer thinkin' like a pirate! And just in time for Doughnut-Breath McStinky to sail in with some helpful shipbuilding tips!

SHIPS AHOY WITH DANIEL

 That's *Captain* Doughnut-Breath McStinky to you, Coconut Kidd! That landlubbing cousin of mine didn't even think that "sloop" was a real word. Back in the Golden Age of Pirates, sloops ruled the high seas!

Wait, you didn't think that "sloop" was a real word either? Well, don't worry, because I'm here to give you the full scoop on sloops—and everything else you need to know to rule the Blowcart Beach challenge!

Thar She Blows

Golden Age pirates used ships that were small and quick to sneak up on bigger boats and steal their loot. Some flew a black flag with skull and crossbones, called a Jolly Roger, to make them look extra tough and scary. They didn't have engines to propel their ships in the water, instead using the power of the wind.

Pirate ships captured wind power with the help of tall masts and large sails. A sail connects to the top and bottom of the mast, puffing out in the middle. When the kinetic (or moving) energy of the wind blows into a sail and the sail puffs out, the energy turns into a force that pushes the boat forward through the water. Remember the boats in the paintings we found in the cave? They all had billowing sails—wind power in action!

The Scoop on Sloops, Schooners, and Barques

Every pirate ship had masts and sails, but not every pirate ship was the same.

Sloops are small, speedy ships with only one mast. With its compact size and big, billowy sail, the sloop was one of the fastest boats on the sea. Pirates loved them because of their ability to zip around in battle and to hide or escape into shallow water.

Schooners were also pirate favorites. With one sail in the front and another in back, these double-masted ships collected twice as much wind as sloops did. Like sloops, schooners gave  pirates the speed they needed to attack treasure-filled ships—and to escape after the robbery.

Barques are bigger than sloops and schooners, with three or more masts, so they so they couldn't go as fast or hide as well in shallow water. But big barques could carry more pirates and more cannons—and most importantly, more treasure!

THE WHEEL DEAL WITH KIMANI

Um, Daniel? What about all the landlubbers out there? Since many of you don't have an ocean handy at home, you can sail your pirate ship across the floor using wheels and axles. It's the same rolling technology that my friends and I used to sail our blowcart across the beach.

The **wheel and axle** is a simple machine that makes it waaaaaaay easier to move things across the ground. Before wheels were invented back in 3200 BC, people had to drag and carry stuff from place to place—or get a strong animal

to carry it for them. Then one day an ancient engineer figured out she could attach a round object (called a wheel) to a rod (called an axle) and it would twist around and around with almost no effort at all. This genius discovery led to the invention of wheelbarrows, ox-pulled carts, horse-drawn carriages, and eventually modern cars and trucks. The wheel was one of the most—if not the most—game-changing invention in the history of the world!

With the help of the wheels and axles my friends and I made out of bamboo poles and wagon wheels, we were able to build a **go-cart** that could easily move heavy barrels across the cave. When we added a sail made out of a canvas painting, we turned our go-cart into a **blow-cart** and went sailing across the beach!

Now that you know the wheel deal, Joy—I mean, Coconut Kidd will help you create your own blowcart.

THE JOY OF DESIGNING YOUR PIRATE SHIP BLOWCART

Build your own sloop, schooner, or barque—it's up to you! Here's what you'll need on deck for this exciting challenge.

Note: You might not use all of the materials in your final design. The engineering process is all about trying and testing out different designs and combinations of materials. You might even try out other materials that are not on this list!

Supplies

- Start and Finish signs (download and print at www.challenge-island.com/books)
- Duct tape
- Pencil and blank paper

- Scissors
- 4 (5-by-8-inch) index cards or pieces of cardboard
- 4 straight straws
- 4 white mint Lifesaver candies
- Play-Doh (or similar clay)
- 4 bendy straws
- 4 pieces of plain paper
- Jolly Roger flag (download and print at www.challenge-island.com/books) or your own designed flag

Set the STEAM Scene!

Find an open area with a hard floor, like the kitchen or a hallway. At one end, tape down the Start sign on the floor. Walk 10 steps away from the starting line and tape down the Finish sign. This is your racetrack for your blowcart. Later on you will add some treasure slime to the finish line.

Sketch Your Design

Now it's time to draw your ideas for your wind-powered pirate ship. Use the pencil and sketch out your design on the blank paper. How many sails will it have? How big will they be? Where will you put them to make sure they catch as much wind as possible?

Next, think about your wheels and axles. How will you attach them to your boat? How will you make sure they roll straight and don't fly off?

As you sketch your design, think about the ships you saw in the book and the lessons that my friends and I learned while engineering our blowcart.

Build Your Pirate Ship Blowcart!

Let's start building! Don't worry if your actual ship ends up looking different from your sketch. Making tweaks and changes along the way is all part of the process. Here are the steps my friends and I used to build our awesome wind-powered blowcart:

1. Design the body. Use an index card for the body of your boat. You might want to fold up the sides of the card to

make your ship more aerodynamic.

2. Attach the axles. Tape two straight straws across the bottom of your ship's body. The ends of the straws should poke out past the sides of the card, just like the bamboo poles poked out from our blowcart. Make sure your axles are taped on straight so your ship will sail straight.

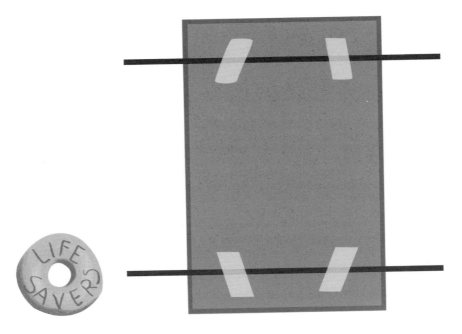

3. Put on the wheels. Slide the Lifesaver wheels onto the straws. Put a bit of Play-Doh or clay on the ends of the straws so the Lifesavers don't slip off. Each wheel should be able to spin freely on its axle without getting stuck on the side of the index card. If a wheel gets stuck, fold up the sides of the card a bit more. Give your blowcart a push to make sure it rolls nicely.

4. Make the masts. Use straight or bendy straws to create the masts. Secure them to the boat using duct tape, clay, or both. If you're building a sloop, you need one mast. If you're building a schooner, you need two masts—one in front and one in back.

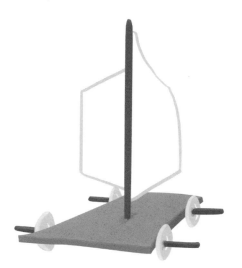

5. Attach the sails. Good sails are the secret to pirate ship–building success. My friends and I made our sails out of painting canvases, but you can make yours out of paper and index cards. Remember how we caught more wind and went faster with a bigger sail? That might help you out too. We also found it was best to keep the bottom of our sail close to the body of the boat so we didn't lose wind underneath the sail.

6. Check the sails. As you're building, test your sails by blowing on them. Does your ship take off or stay put? Experiment with different sizes, numbers, and placements of sails. There is no right or wrong way to design your sails.

7. Give it some personality. Make a Jolly Roger flag for your ship, or add your own cool design to the sails. Invent a pirate ship name and write it somewhere on the ship.

8. Test and improve it. Place your ship on the starting line. Blow hard into the sail with a straw or your mouth. How long did it take to blow your ship to the finish line? Did

you notice anything slowing your ship down? Can you see any way to speed it up? Make changes to the sails and masts and see if they improve the ship's speed.

9. Race to the treasure slime! When you are happy with your ship design, it's time to put it to the test. Invite friends or family to build their own ships and race against each another.

DAVINCI'S ART ATTACK

Blow me down, ye scallywags, you built some mighty fine clippers! True STEAM captains ye are!

As you may know, the A in STEAM stands for Art. Or Arrrrrrrrrrt, as pirates like to say. Most people think of art as something you see. But art can engage *any* of the five senses: sight, hearing, touch, smell, and taste.

For the last part of your Blowcart Beach challenge, you will be mixing up a super STEAMy slime concoction. Notice how it stimulates your different senses. *See* how shiny and colorful it looks. *Feel* how it squishes and stretches between your fingers. *Hear* how it pops in your hands when you squeeze it. *Smell* the gooey, gluey scent!

Make Pirate Treasure Slime

This recipe contains borax powder, which is made from the same kind of borax crystals me mateys found at the pond. (If you would rather make slime without borax powder, use our alternate recipe from Book 1 of the Challenge Island series, *The Bridge to Sharktooth Island*.) So roll up your sleeves, because you'll be mixing up a sensationally slimy treasure!

Supplies

- 1 big bowl
- 1 small bowl
- Mixing spoons
- ½ cup clear school glue
- ½ cup cold or room temperature water
- Gold glitter
- ½ cup *warm* water
- ¼ teaspoon borax powder
- Playful pirate booty such as craft gems and plastic coins and pearls

Directions

1. In a big bowl, stir together the clear school glue and ½ cup cold or room temperature water.
2. Stir the gold glitter into the water-glue mixture.
3. In a small bowl, make a borax solution by stirring ½ cup warm water with the borax powder.
4. Add the borax solution a little at a time to the big bowl with the glittery glue mixture. You may not need to add

the whole amount, so keep stirring and adding the borax solution until you get the slimy consistency you like.

5. Mix in your pirate booty into the bowl and stir to combine.

6. Take the slime out of the bowl and squish it around in your hands until it's not sticky. Avast ye, this is your Pirate Treasure Slime—keep it safe!

KIMANI'S SLIMY SCIENCE

Captain Wei taught us that the more we understand the secrets of science, the more magic we can create. In the case of slime, the magic takes place through a colossally cool chemical reaction between different substances.

Every substance in the world is made up of zillions of itty-bitty, teeny-weeny parts called *molecules*. In glue, those molecules really like each other, so they hold hands with their besties. This hand-holding creates chains of molecules called *polymers*. Think of the polymers as strands of spaghetti. These polymer chains slip and slide past one another, keeping the glue in a sticky, liquid state.

But when you add in another substance called borate ions, a chemical reaction happens that looks like magic—but really it's just science at work. The borate ions activate the polymers to *crosslink*. So the individual strands of spaghetti link up with one another and become connected. The crosslinked bonds between the strands are weak, however, so the polymer chains can still slip and slide